MOTHER GOOSE
NURSERY RHYMES

Seeing Colors

with

MOTHER GOOSE

Compiled by Stephanie Hedlund
Illustrated by Jeremy Tugeau

magic
wagon

visit us at www.abdopublishing.com

Published by Magic Wagon, a division of the ABDO Group, 8000 West 78th Street, Edina, Minnesota 55439. Copyright © 2011 by Abdo Consulting Group, Inc. International copyrights reserved in all countries. All rights reserved. No part of this book may be reproduced in any form without written permission from the publisher.

Looking Glass Library™ is a trademark and logo of Magic Wagon.

Printed in the United States of America, North Mankato, Minnesota.
102010
012011

This book contains at least 10% recycled materials.

Compiled by Stephanie Hedlund
Illustrations by Jeremy Tugeau
Edited by Rochelle Baltzer
Cover and interior layout by Abbey Fitzgerald

Library of Congress Cataloging-in-Publication Data

Seeing colors with Mother Goose / compiled by Stephanie Hedlund ; illustrated by Jeremy Tugeau.
    v. cm. -- (Mother Goose nursery rhymes)
  Contents: Nursery rhymes about colors -- Something old, something new -- Three gray geese -- Roses are red -- Hoddley, poddley -- A red sky -- If you love me -- Mary had a pretty bird -- There was a little green house -- Little Betty Blue -- Red stockings, blue stockings -- Little Jack Horner -- Hector Protector -- The brown owl.
  ISBN 978-1-61641-146-6
  1. Nursery rhymes. 2. Colors--Juvenile poetry. 3. Children's poetry. [1. Nursery rhymes. 2. Color--Poetry.] I. Hedlund, Stephanie F., 1977- II. Tugeau, Jeremy, ill. III. Mother Goose.
  PZ8.3.S45105 2011
  398.8 [E]--dc22
                    2010024698

Contents

Nursery Rhymes
About Colors

Since early days, people have created rhymes to teach and entertain children. Since they were often said in a nursery, they became known as nursery rhymes. In the 1700s, these nursery rhymes were collected and published to share with parents and other adults.

Some of these collections were named after Mother Goose. Mother Goose didn't actually exist, but there are many stories about who she could be. Her rhymes were so popular, people began using *Mother Goose rhymes* to refer to most nursery rhymes.

Since the 1600s, nursery rhymes have come from many sources. The meanings of the rhymes have been lost, but they are an important form of folk language. Nursery rhymes about colors introduce readers to the colors all around them.

Something Old, Something New

Something old, something new,
Something borrowed, something blue,
And a penny in her shoe.

Three Gray Geese

Three gray geese in a green field grazing;
Gray were the geese and green was the grazing.

Roses Are Red

Roses are red,

Violets are blue,

Sugar is sweet

And so are you!

Hoddley, Poddley

Hoddley, poddley, puddles and fogs,

Cats are to marry poodle dogs;

Cats in blue jackets and dogs in red hats,

What will become of the mice and the rats?

A Red Sky

A red sky at night is a shepherd's delight;

A red sky in the morning is a shepherd's warning.

If You Love Me

If you love me, love me true,

Send me a ribbon, and let it be blue.

If you hate me, let it be seen,

Send me a ribbon, a ribbon of green.

Mary Had a
Pretty Bird

18

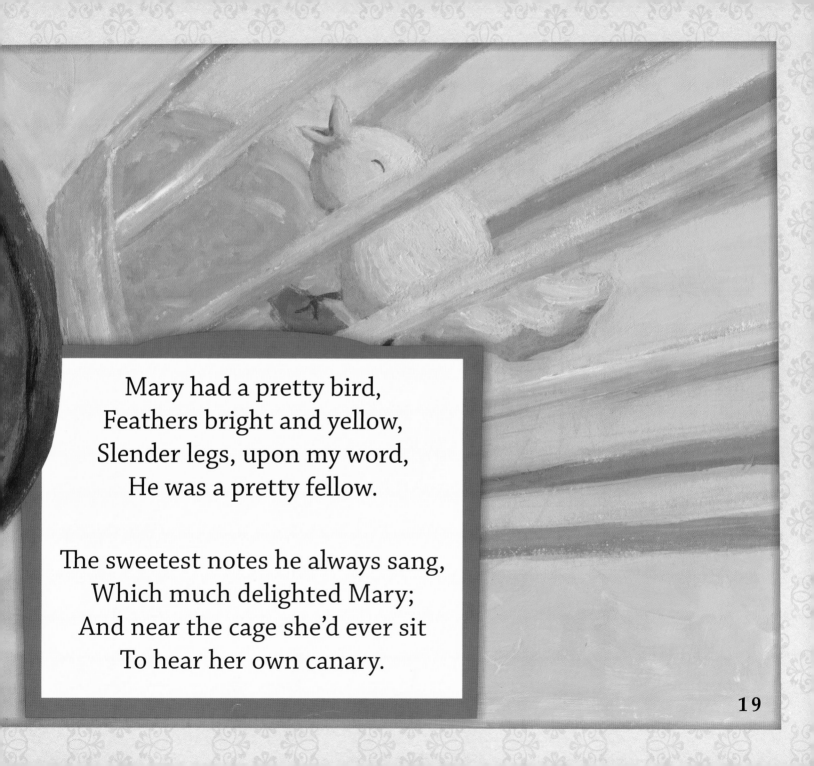

Mary had a pretty bird,
Feathers bright and yellow,
Slender legs, upon my word,
He was a pretty fellow.

The sweetest notes he always sang,
Which much delighted Mary;
And near the cage she'd ever sit
To hear her own canary.

There Was a Little Green House

There was a little green house,

And in the little green house

There was a little brown house,

And in the little brown house

There was a little yellow house,

And in the little yellow house,

There was a little white house,

And in the little white house

There was a little heart.

Little Betty Blue

Little Betty Blue lost her holiday shoe;
What can little Betty do?
Give her another to match the other,
And then she may walk out in two.

Red Stockings, Blue Stockings

Red stockings, blue stockings,
  Shoes tied up with silver;
A red rosette upon my breast
And a gold ring on my finger.

Little Jack Horner

Little Jack Horner

Sat in a corner,

Eating a Christmas pie;

He put in his thumb

And pulled out a plum

And said, "What a good boy am I."

Hector Protector

Hector Protector was dressed all in green;

Hector Protector was sent to the queen.

The queen did not like him,

No more did the king;

So Hector Protector was sent back again.

The Brown Owl

The Brown Owl sits in the ivy bush,
And she looketh wondrous wise,
With a horny beak beneath her cowl,
And a pair of large round eyes.

She sat all day on the selfsame spray,
From sunrise till sunset;
And the dim grey light, it was all too bright
For the Owl to see in yet.

"Jenny Owlet, Jenny Owlet," said a merry little bird.
"They say you're wondrous wise;
But I don't think you see, though you're looking at *me*
With your large, round, shining eyes.

But night came soon, and the pale white moon
Rolled high up in the skies;
And the great Brown Owl flew away in her cowl,
With her large, round, shining eyes.

Glossary

breast – another word for chest.

cowl – a cape or hood.

graze – to feed on land covered in grass.

rosette – an ornament made of material and shaped to look like a rose.

shepherd – a person who tends sheep.

slender – thin.

stocking – a knit sock.

wondrous – something wonderful.

Web Sites

To learn more about nursery rhymes, visit ABDO Group online at **www.abdopublishing.com**. Web sites about nursery rhymes are featured on our Book Links page. These links are routinely monitored and updated to provide the most current information available.